M000217718

Jacked

Carrie Mac

orca soundings

ORCA BOOK PUBLISHERS

For Jasper, Mister Bad

Copyright © 2009 Carrie Mac

Library and Archives Canada Cataloguing in Publication

Mac, Carrie, 1975-
Jacked / Carrie Mac.

(Orca soundings)
ISBN 978-1-55469-185-2 (bound).--ISBN 978-1-55469-184-5 (pbk.)

I. Title. II. Series: Orca soundings

PS8625.A23J32 2009   jC813'.6   C2009-902577-9

Summary: Zane is carjacked and forced to drive by a masked gunman.

First published in the United States, 2009
Library of Congress Control Number: 2009927570

Orca Book Publishers gratefully acknowledges the support for
its publishing programs provided by the following agencies: the
Government of Canada through the Book Publishing Industry
Development Program and the Canada Council for the Arts, and the
Province of British Columbia through the BC Arts Council and
the Book Publishing Tax Credit.

Cover design by Teresa Bubela
Cover photography by Getty Images

ORCA BOOK PUBLISHERS
PO Box 5626, STN. B
VICTORIA, BC CANADA
V8R 6S4

ORCA BOOK PUBLISHERS
PO Box 468
CUSTER, WA USA
98240-0468

www.orcabook.com
Printed and bound in Canada.
Printed on 100% PCW recycled paper.
12 11 10 09 • 4 3 2 1

Chapter One

7:00 AM
When I show up for my shift, I find Dorkus Roboticus exactly where I left him last night, on the tall stool behind the cash register. I swear he doesn't even get off that thing to pee. He probably just pisses into an empty pop bottle. I guess he doesn't really have to move. He can reach the till, and the night window,

and even the cigarettes, which is pretty much the only thing people want in the middle of the night. I asked him once what he did when someone wanted him to grab them a bag of chips or a liter of oil that he can't reach from his stool. He looked at me with big blank eyes.

"They don't."

I wouldn't ask him either. He's as creepy as he is weird. I call him Dorkus Roboticus because he moves like a robot. And because he spends every nightshift making up crossword puzzles. Hence the dork factor.

"What the hell do you do with those?" I ask him as I push open the door. I grab the last crossword just as he is about to put it away. *Four across, 1964 zombie beach classic. Eight down, triangular medieval torture tool.*

He says nothing. Only stares.

"Alrighty then." I drop the crossword. He's that kind of creepy. I slide the paper across the counter to him and then go to put on the coffee.

"How was your night?" I ask him this every morning too, because awkward silence is just that. Awkward. I don't care if I have to fill it all by myself. I will.

He shrugs as he slides off the stool.

"Float's okay?"

He nods.

"So, Dorkus." The coffee done, I pour myself an enormous cup of it and doctor it with a handful of flavored creamers and six packets of sugar. I grab a stale donut from the display case and join him behind the till. "Got any big plans for the day?"

He slowly turns his head as he lifts the strap of his man purse over his head. He wears it across his chest, like that makes it any less girlified.

"Huh?" He blinks at me with his crusty, bloodshot eyes.

"Plans," I repeat. "Are you *doing* any-thing today. I am attempting small talk.

You know this phrase? Small talk? So again, I ask…are you doing anything today?"

"Sleep." He shrugs. "I dunno."

"Well, rock on." I take a big swig of coffee. "Just rock on, man."

"Yeah." He shuffles a few steps toward the door, then stops. He stands there for a long moment and then turns back using a series of painstakingly small movements. Watching him makes me want to take up competitive running. Jesus! "Oh," he says, "Kozlov is coming in at noon. Have fun."

I don't know what bothers me more, the fact that Dorkus Roboticus just had the longest conversation he'd ever had with me, or the fact the boss is coming. Mr. Kozlov is scary. He was a champion boxer in Russia before he came here, and he still trains every day. In fact, I think that's all he does every day. That, and drive around in his hummer with his two enormous

Rottweiler dogs hanging their big blocky heads out the rear window.

It occurs to me while I'm tidying the chocolate-bar display that maybe Kozlov isn't coming at all, and this was Dorkus's idea of a joke. I think about the likelihood, but keep on straightening up. I sweep; I stock up the coolers; I put out the baking that has been sitting outside since 4:00 AM; I wipe a week's worth of fingerprints off the glass door. I even clean the bathroom. I hate cleaning the bathroom. This is how I know that I'm not taking a chance that Dorkus might be messing with me. I'd rather be prepared than have Kozlov come in and find a million reasons to fire me, or worse, rough me up in an impromptu one-sided boxing match.

Chapter Two

9:00 AM
The morning passes slowly. Customers drift in, one after the other, like so many gas-guzzling zombies. I try to think of something other than Kozlov. I think about food. That usually works. Or sex, but that would be a problem if a little old lady wanted me to come outside and check her oil. Stick to food.

But then I get a craving. Not just any craving that you can put off until later, but a true vise-grip sort of craving that will not go away. The deli at the end of the block makes these wicked breakfast burritos. It's all I can think about, which is good, because Kozlov's visit slides to the back of my mind. The other great thing about the breakfast burrito is that the girl who makes them is smoking hot. And super nice. And she actually talks to me. Maybe flirts even. But I don't know. Whatever flirting is. That would be the sort of thing you could ask a best friend, but seeing as I'm just a garden-variety loner, I'm on my own.

Anyway, she's really cute, with these big perky tits that I just want to grab at every time I see her. And an eensy little waist that I just want to—

Focus on the burrito, Zane! Not the girl. Food, not sex.

Okay, I know it's not good to just up and leave the station for even five minutes, but I have to have one of those burritos. And a fortifying glance at Melissa, the burrito girl. I've done this before and never gotten caught. I'll take my car and go through the pick-up window, which makes it way faster. Kozlov isn't coming until noon. I'll be there and back way before he's supposed to show up.

9:15 AM

I grab my keys, tape up a little note that says I'll be back in five minutes and then lock the door behind me.

I pull out of the parking lot and wait for a break in the traffic before turning onto the street. I'm looking left, when suddenly I hear a car door open. It's a long stupid second before I realize that it's one of *my* car doors. The passenger door, to be exact.

Confused, I turn to look. There's a masked man in the passenger seat, pointing a gun at me.

A masked man.

With a gun.

In my car.

"What the hell?" I take my hands off the steering wheel and stick them up, surrender-style. It seems the appropriate thing to do.

"Drive!" He waves the gun at me.

So I put my hands back on the steering wheel. Now *this* seems to be the appropriate thing to do.

"Who are you?" I force the words out of my mouth, which has quickly become full of cement, or so it feels.

I grip the steering wheel and stare at him.

"I said *drive!*" He jams the gun into my temple so hard that my head knocks into the window. "Gas pedal, right foot. Now!"

The black ski mask entirely covers his face, except for the mouth and eye holes. He's also wearing a black hoodie, the hood pulled up. Jeans. Sneakers. It occurs to me that this could be Dorkus Roboticus, in a valiant attempt to get back at me for teasing him about his crossword puzzles.

"Dorkus, if that's you, then I'm impressed." I nod, work up a smile. I clap, that slow, tacky clap you see in the movies when the bystanders have to admit that the underdog has finally triumphed. "Very well done." I keep clapping. "I like the ski mask. Nice touch."

I can hear the guy breathing heavily, his gun still at my temple.

"I said *drive*." The fabric of the mask lifts a little when he talks. There's a click as he cocks the gun. "Drive."

I do as he says.

Chapter Three

9:20 AM

I pull into traffic as cautiously as a little old lady who can barely see above the dash. It's not that I'm a nervous driver. Not at all. I've had a lot speeding tickets, and the only reason I don't have more is that the next time I'll get my license taken away. I still speed, don't get me wrong. I just speed selectively. Smartly.

But right this minute, I do feel like a little old lady. My knuckles are white from gripping the wheel so hard. My fingers are stiff. My arms are shaking. My right foot—which is usually very happy being on the gas pedal—is trembling so bad that I can hardly keep a decent speed at all. I can feel my pulse throbbing in my neck. In that vein that always bulges up when I'm pissed off. Or scared. I am both, only the anger seems a very distant second to the fear.

I chance a quick glance over at the guy. He's got his eyes locked on me and doesn't miss it.

"What?"

I look back at the road, hands at ten and two. "Nothing."

"Good."

His voice is deeper than mine. I'm guessing he's older than me. Maybe middle-aged, even. He's definitely not

Dorkus Roboticus. Although the hoodie kind of makes him look younger, like maybe in his twenties or something. Maybe Dorkus got a friend to do this. Maybe this is a prank after all. Just because the guy isn't Dorkus doesn't mean that Dorkus isn't behind it.

"I bet he paid you to do this, didn't he?" I keep my eyes on the road as I talk. "It's okay, I won't go to the cops or anything. It's funny. I get it. Very funny. He got me good. Ha ha ha."

The guy says nothing. He's lowered the gun now so that no one can see it from the outside of the car, even though all my windows (except the windshield) are tinted. He's resting it on the emergency brake, so it's aimed at my waist.

"Turn right."

"Here?" The intersection is right in front of us. I don't turn. Not because I'm trying to be an ass, but because I genuinely wasn't sure if he meant this one or the one coming up.

"I said turn!" The gun comes back up, poking at my cheek now. "Why didn't you turn?"

"I wasn't sure—"

"Just shut the hell up and go back."

All right. I glance over my shoulder and in the rearview mirror before yanking the wheel hard to the left to do a U-turn.

"Not like that!" He spins, looking to see who's around. "If you're trying to get the cops on our ass, you'll be sorry."

No one saw us. I wished they had. This is a main road, and you'd think there'd be a patrol car or two around. But no. There's hardly any traffic at all. And the tinted windows don't help. No one will wonder why some guy is wearing a ski mask on a warm spring day. I get into the turning lane and make what is now a right-hand turn onto the feeder road that goes to the highway. I'm really, really hoping he's not taking us onto the highway.

"What about money?" I ask.

"What about it?"

"We could stop at an ATM. I could get you some money." I don't tell him that there's only seventeen dollars in my bank account, but I figure if we stop, I can try to get away. "Cash."

"I don't care about money. Just drive."

Chapter Four

9:25 AM

We pass the park, and I don't slow down for the playground zone. He doesn't notice, but neither does anyone else. Still no cops. Why are they everywhere when you don't want them and then nowhere to be found when the fit hits the shan?

The fit hits the shan. My mom says that all the time. It annoys me, or it usually does. But right now, I'd give anything to go home and hear her weird little sayings. Tell her about this crazy guy who tried to carjack me, but I got away. Only that's not how the story is playing out.

"You want my car?" I say, almost friendly. "You can have it."

This takes a lot for me. This must mean that I think I'm in real danger, although it hasn't sunk in quite yet. I love my car. It's just a piece of crap Honda Civic from eleven million years ago, but it's *my* car. *I* found it in the paper for $400. *I* paid for the tow to bring it to the shop at the school. *I* worked on it for two whole semesters before it would actually run well. I nursed this baby back from the dead. This car and I go way back. I could easily say that my car is my best friend. I named the car Vicky when the refurbished engine finally turned over for the first time. My shop teacher thought

I named the car Vicky because it's a Civic, but it's for Victorious. I hope Vicky will understand. I hope she'll forgive me when the cops find her burned-out carcass on a lonely dirt road somewhere.

"What do you say, man?" I risk another glance at him. He's still clutching the gun. Still staring at me. But his eyes—from what I can see through the mask—seem far away. He's probably high.

"What?"

Of course he's high. Who would pull a stunt like this unless they were smoked?

Probably meth, just my luck. I've seen the TV shows. I know how easily tweakers can flip out.

And I doubt a meth-head will listen to reason. "My car," I say again. "You can have my car. Vicky will understand."

"Who the hell is Vicky?" His eyebrows scrunch into all that I can see of a frown. "Someone you're supposed to pick up?"

What would he care if it was?

"My car. She's called Vicky." We're only a few blocks from the on-ramp to the highway. "Look, I can pull over right here and hand over the keys, man. No hard feelings. Just take good care of her. She has an external starter." I point to the button by the ignition. "I had to put that in. I can't remember if that was before or after I put in the new clutch, but whatever—"

"Shut up."

But I can't. I'm nervous and freaked out and cannot shut up. "You have to push that as you turn the key and depress the clutch. All at the same time. Got it?"

"Did I or did I not say *shut up*?"

Got it—shut up and drive. Understood.

"I don't want your stupid car."

But then my nerves get the better of me, and I start babbling again. "And there's no heater." I show him the hole in the dash where the controls used to be. "I took it out because I thought there was a loose connection, but that's not the problem. Still doesn't work." I cannot stop talking. I'm scared of this guy. And I'm scared of getting onto the highway with him and going who the hell knows where. And so I keep babbling like an idiot. "So if it gets really cold and the windows frost over, you have to scrape from the inside too. There's a scraper in the backseat. And there's a little space heater back there too. You can plug it into the cigarette lighter. Doesn't work great. But enough to keep your ass from freezing to the seat."

"I don't want your car."

It occurs to me that if I was this guy, and he was me, I might've shot off his head by now. Just to get him to shut up. I tell myself this, along with strict instructions to SHUT UP. But it's no use. The verbal diarrhea keeps coming.

"She's not as complicated as I make her out to be. She's a good car. Besides the crappy tint job. I did it myself, and the film was a total bitch. But, really. You can have her. Honest. Like I said, I won't call the cops or nothing. You and me. Our little secret. No one has to know about this."

"Go west."

The highway signs are coming up. I get into the lane that'll merge onto the westbound lanes.

"You don't want money. You don't want my car. C'mon, man…" I'm getting desperate. I do not want to get on the highway with this maniac. We could end up anywhere. No one would know where to look for me. What if he's some kind of sadist and I end up dismembered, my torso in one ditch, my legs in another and my head in his freezer? What if I never see my mom again? What if I never get to tell her that it's actually kind of cute when she says *the fit hits the shan*? What if I go missing and everyone assumes I've run away when really I'm being held captive by some lunatic in his underground dungeon, being tortured and violated?

What if that one time I had sex with Brenda Mitford behind the concession stand at Cultus Lake is the only sex I'll ever have? What if I die before having real sex and not just a drunken disaster that ruined my friendship with a girl who'd been my buddy since third grade? What if I never get to tell Brenda that I wished we hadn't done it, or not like that anyway? "What do you want?"

"I want you to head west."

I turn on my signal light. "West?"

"That's what I said, isn't it?"

We merge onto highway traffic. It's still early for a Saturday, but there's lots of traffic on the highway anyway. Four lanes of it, in fact. "You want me to stay here, or go into the commuter lane?" Because there's two of us, we can go in the high-occupancy lane.

Why can't I just SHUT UP?

"What?" he says.

"Which lane do you want to be in?" I ask.

"I don't care. Just drive. Normally."

Be quiet, I tell myself. Just be quiet.

We pass the exit that goes to the Agriplex. There's a big rodeo going on there this weekend. I can see the rodeo grounds from the highway, and a cloud of dust rising up from the bullring. I'd rather be riding a badass angry bull, trying for my eight seconds, than stuck in this car with a homicidal freak.

"What do you want?" I can't help but ask again. I am afraid of the answer. Terrified. But I want to know. Need to know. Not that he'll tell me the truth. He has a gun. He can tell me whatever he wants.

"A driver," he says. He sets the gun on his thigh, still clutching it tightly. "I want you to drive me somewhere. I just want you to drive."

Chapter Five

9:31 AM

We've been on the highway for three minutes now, and he hasn't said another word. I glance over at him, and he seems to be tweaking on something. He's kind of mumbling to himself, shaking his head a little. A few moments later he lets out a quiet moan. I think about asking if he's all right, but I figure I better not.

As for the gun, it's still resting on his left thigh, the barrel pointed at me. If it went off, the bullet would launch right into my stomach. I'd probably die instantly. Especially if he got an artery. That'd be better than slow and painful.

But if he shoots me while I'm driving, I'll crash the car. And he'd die too. He wouldn't do that, would he? He said he wanted a driver. I can do that. The driver has to live, right? How else can I drive? But what if he's suicidal? You've got to be, to some degree, to pull a stunt like this, in broad daylight, with a gun.

The next time I glance over, the gun has slid down a little and is aimed right at my crotch. I imagine the blast, the searing pain. I wince.

He glances over, the whites of his eyes standing out against the black wool. "What?"

I shake my head, not wanting to give him any ideas. But the gun stays aimed at my crotch, and concern for my reproductive organ gets the better of me.

"Could you just move the gun...even just a little?" I point at the gun. Then I point to my crotch. "You can shoot me through the heart, but please spare the package."

"I'm not—," he starts to say, exasperated. "Fine." He angles the gun upward.

9:42 AM

I know where every speed trap is along this highway. Why? Because I've gotten a ticket at half of them and talked my way out of a ticket at the other half of them. The cops hide in the Emergency Vehicles Only lanes that join the two directions of highway. The trick is that each of these lanes is announced by a little white sign. Slow down at the sign, you'll appear nice and law-abiding when your vehicle comes into the radar range. I've been speeding between these signs, and then slowing down…just like I always do.

But now I wonder…why? *Why*? When I could keep on speeding and hopefully get pulled over.

This is more of a sacrifice than it sounds.

I was told last time that if I got one more speeding ticket, my license will be taken away. Just for speeding! Have I ever gotten into an accident? Ever? No. Not even a parking-lot fender bender. Have I ever even *caused* an accident? I'll bet no. I'm an excellent driver. I just have a slightly heavy foot.

I have ten speeding tickets. Three of which I haven't paid for. I got a letter in the mail from the DMV telling me what a bad person I am and that, as a new driver, I'm shirking my responsibility and not appreciating the privilege of driving.

Who the hell says *shirk*? And since when did the DMV send out letters that read like a letter from the teacher telling your mother how you're messing up your future by flunking so royally at math. I would know. I've had a few of those letters.

So the choice is as follows…keep going along with the crazed madman sitting not two feet away from me with a loaded weapon, or risk losing my driver's license for a year. It will be a long year.

I decide to try to talk him out of whatever this is, one last time.

"You got a name?"

"No."

"Something I can call you?"

"What?" He looks over, his ski mask a little tight on his face, so his eyes look squashed. He straightens it. "So you can try some bullshit *CSI* thing where you try to make me see you as a 'human being' so I won't hurt you?" He air-quotes "human being" with the fingers of one hand.

"And why not?" I say, pissed off. "I kind of like breathing on a regular basis."

"You don't have to call me anything." There's a catch in his throat, like he's about to cough. Or cry.

"You all right?"

"Just drive." He turns his face to the window, which is pretty stupid kidnapper behavior if you ask me. I could grab his gun. Easily. But then, as if he's reading my mind, he grips it tighter and says, "Don't even bother trying."

"I'll call you Bud."

"Whatever."

"Bud seems suitable for—" One of those emergency pullouts is coming up. I put gentle pressure on the gas. Increase the speed slowly so he won't notice. "For a guy like you."

"Right!" He says with a snort. "Because you know me so well!"

I'm way over the limit as the pullout comes into view.

Please let there be a cop.

Please let me get pulled over.

Please. Please. Please.

The knoll they usually tuck the cop car behind is grassy, dotted with daffodils…and not a cop in sight.

Crap.

Bud shifts in his seat. "Slow down."

Thankfully, I already had. By the time he had a look at the speedometer, I was just gliding back toward the speed limit anyway.

"Done," I say.

He watches me for a few minutes and then leans his head back. He groans. I can barely hear it, but it's a definite groan.

"You sure you're all right, Bud?"

Up comes the gun. He clicks off the safety. "I'm fine."

"Okay, okay!" I lift one hand off of the steering wheel in a truce. "Sorry."

Chapter Six

9:53 AM
We pass another emergency pullout. I don't have a chance to speed, and it wouldn't have mattered anyway. No cop.

Where the hell are they?

Bud is shaking his head, kind of talking to himself again. Mumbling something. I wonder how long it takes for whatever he's on to wear off? What's the time span for meth? Crack? Heroin? Hell, I don't know what he's on anyway.

We pass a sign announcing yet another emergency pullout. I take my chances and step on the gas. I catch a glimpse of Bud. He doesn't seem to notice. He's still mumbling to himself. I ease the speed ever higher, and then I see it. The glint of the radar gun. The cop in his blazing yellow safety jacket. The cop car parked neatly off to one side, hidden by yet another grassy knoll.

And there it is, the pull-over-now wave. He lowers the radar gun and uses his whole arm to gesture for me to pull over. I slow. Bud lifts his head.

"You did that on purpose!" he says as he looks around for somewhere to tuck the gun. He ends up shoving it down his pants as I steer the car onto the shoulder and to a full stop. As we wait for the cop, Bud leans over and twists my shirt collar in his fist, twisting and twisting until I can hardly breathe.

"One word," he growls. "One weird eye blink. One single, silent *help me* and I will kill you. I swear to God, I will blow your brains all over this car."

9:55 AM

I can see the cop approaching in the rearview mirror. He hasn't got the swagger of a normal cop. He kind of ambles toward the car, like he's got all the time in the world. Personally, I would like him to hurry the hell up.

Bud lets go of my shirt with a shove, and then he turns away and pulls off his ski mask.

"You look at me, I'll shoot you."

"Got it."

He grabs one of my baseball caps off the floor and yanks it down low across his brow. I catch a glimpse before he helps himself to a pair of my sunglasses too. He's got brown hair, and a neck full of zits. And that's all I see. He turns his face to his window.

"Not one word," he reminds me as I roll down my window to talk to the cop.

"Good morning, sir." I widen my eyes, hoping they make me look like I need help.

He doesn't even look at me. He glances down the highway, as if I'm not worthy of his full attention. "Know how fast you were going?"

"No, sir. I do not." Please look at me. I will him to. Dagger my eyes at him. Mentally beg him to look at me. But he doesn't. He's still looking down the highway as he asks for my license and registration.

"License I can do…" Maybe if I pretend that my registration is not in my glove box—

But Bud catches on to what I'm doing. He opens the glove box and pulls out my papers.

"Here you go, officer." He says this in the nicest boy-next-door voice. I would dare look at him, but the thought of his gun keeps me from giving in to the urge.

"Remove your sunglasses," the cop tells him.

I grin. Now I've got him.

"Sorry, sir, but I can't." Bud sounds polite, even. Like someone you wouldn't mind your sister dating. "See, I just had an eye-doctor appointment and they put those drops in that make your pupils dilate. That's why Zane is driving me home. I can't drive for two hours. And I really shouldn't take the glasses off."

"Gotcha." The cop nods. "I hate those drops."

"No kidding," Bud says.

I wonder when they're going to crack open a beer and discuss the latest football stats.

And then I wonder something different. How does Bud know my name?

10:01 AM

The cop ambles back to his car to check out my license. This is when he finds out that I have so many tickets that this one will cost me my license. This is when he calls for a tow truck, and Bud will have no other option but to play along.

This is when it's all over.

"How do you know my name?"

Bud waits a few long seconds before answering. "It's on your uniform."

"No it's not." My gas-station uniform says *Dwayne*...because I think it's a better name for a guy that works at a gas station. The real Dwayne is in rehab for a bad crack habit. Which got him fired after he faked two robberies with his friends and then split the cash. The cops arrested him, he went to jail and then rehab, and I took his uniform. I wouldn't be surprised if this guy and Dwayne are friends.

"I read it on your registration," Bud amends his story.

"You did not."

Out comes the gun. "You really want to argue with me?"

"Do I know you?"

He shakes his head. "No."

"Then how did you know my name?"

"I told you!" Bud is clearly agitated now. His voice kind of screeches, and there's sweat in the crease at the back of his neck, but still he won't turn and look at me. "I read it."

He did not. I know he didn't. Again, I wonder if somebody is pulling some kind of prank on me. But I don't have any friends, and no enemy would bother going to this much trouble to mess with my head. As twisted as this is, this is a prank befitting a friend. I don't have friends. Unless you count Dorkus Roboticus, and I doubt anyone would.

"Who put you up to this?"

But he doesn't answer. The cop is back at my window, his eyes fixed on my license.

"Looks like your luck has run out," he says.

"Oh?" I ask with as much innocence in my voice as I can muster. "What do you mean, sir?"

"You know very well what I mean. If I give you a ticket today, you lose your license. I'm sure you got the lecture last time you got pulled over. And…" He hands me back my license and registration. Why is he doing this? He should be seizing it! Calling for a tow truck! "*And* you have failed to pay three of those many tickets."

"So…" I can feel a stammer building in my throat. "So-so-so, what now?"

"Well"—the cop leans into the car—"your luck might've run out, but your friend still has a little on the meter. I'm going to let you go today."

"But—" I'm about to protest, but I realize that would be very stupid with a crazed gunman in the car, prank or no prank. The gun is real.

"Thank you very much, officer." I can practically hear Bud grinning at the cop. I don't need to turn to look at him to know that's what he's doing. What a two-faced prick.

"Well, you just get the both of you home safe," the cop says to me, finally looking at me in the eye. I'm so baffled that I forget to give him the help-me-I'm-being-held-against-my-will-by-a-crazed-gunman look. And when I remember, the cop is already looking wistfully down the highway. "Yep," he says, agreeing with no one in particular, "you two just consider this your lucky day that I don't want to file the paperwork involved in taking this guy here off the road." He cocks a finger at me and then winks. "I was once your age. I can appreciate a thing or two."

"Well, thank you, officer." Bud is just oozing loveliness. What a brown-nosing little lunatic. "I appreciate it. And Zane does too."

He pats the roof of the car. "Well, you boys take care now."

And he ambles back to his little radar station, gun angled at the highway.

10:04 AM

Out comes the gun, off come the hat and glasses, back on with the ski mask. Bud has magically transformed back into the drug-addled thug I know and do not love.

"You try something like that again, and I will aim for your dick." He presses the gun into my side as he tells me this. "No matter where we are, or what it takes, I will shoot your dick right off. Got it?"

I nod.

My dick shrivels with fear.

I will the cop to come back to the car. I will him to change his mind and want me off the road. I will him to realize that he's made a terrible mistake and should teach me a lesson once and for all.

"Drive." Bud growls the word at me. I start the car. And then it hits me like a knuckle-duster left hook to the jaw. I am thankful. So very, very thankful to still have my license. I've just proven that it's worse to lose your license for one year than be forced to drive to an undisclosed location by a masked gunman who might go postal at any moment.Something must be wrong with me. That's just not right. Is it?

Chapter Seven

10:15 AM

I'm guessing we're headed to the city. There are a bunch of suburby towns before we get there, but for some reason, I'm thinking we're going all the way into the city. Maybe I'm thinking this so that I won't freak out when we just keep driving and driving. Or maybe it's because the city is where you get drugs.

At least, I think so. I know you can get drugs in our town, but it seems more city-like to go right downtown and get them off the street like you see in TV reality shows about people whose lives have been ruined by addiction.

"Take the next exit," Bud says, interrupting my thoughts with the first words he's spoken to me since threatening to shoot my dick off.

So maybe I was wrong. We're only at Langley. Still a good forty-five minutes until the city.

"What for?"

He doesn't answer me.

"That's okay," I say as I switch lanes. "I didn't really expect you to answer me or anything."

Still, he says nothing.

"But you might want to let me know which way you want me to go at the stop sign."

He taps the window, pointing right.

"I'll take that as a right." I find it bizarre to be receiving the silent treatment from my captor. But whatever. At least he's not telling me how he's going to take me to an abandoned industrial site and brutalize me before savoring my death as he puts the gun to my head or a knife to my throat.

"Pull into the gas station."

He speaks! I just about say those words, in that tone, but decide not to.

"Fill up the car," he adds as I'm about to park in front of the convenience store. "Don't you think I can see the gauge from here?"

It's true. The gauge shows less than a quarter tank. I hadn't thought of running out of gas as a way of getting out of this. He's smart. I pull up beside a pump instead.

"I've only got seventeen dollars in the bank, and maybe ten in my wallet."

"So when you were offering me money, you were lying."

"Guilty."

He thinks for a minute. "Only put in ten bucks. We might need the rest of the money later."

"For what?"

He doesn't answer. I undo my seatbelt and reach for the door, all the while looking down the road. I've already decided not to make a run for the store. Instead I'm going to hightail it down the road, screaming and yelling my head off for someone to help me. I pull the door handle, hear the familiar creak as I open it, but then he stops me with the gun at my back, discreetly held below the dash so no one will notice.

"You try to run, I'll shoot."

"Got it." I leave my hand on the door. Raise the other in a half truce. He presses the barrel harder against my spine. I hear him take off his ski mask and don the hat and sunglasses.

"I mean it."

"Okay." I arch away from the gun. "I get it."

"First, you're going to get the gas." He jabs the gun at my back again. "Then we're going to the bathroom. Together."

He's not going to—

He's not—

I stare at him. What do I do now?

"Not for that!" he says, reading my mind. "God. What are you, some kind of pervert? No way. I just have to take a piss."

Something about him suddenly sounds familiar.

"Who are you?" I half turn to get a look at him.

"Don't look at me!"

"I know you, don't I?"

"Gas. Now."

I think of everyone I've ever met. Scrolling through them like so many online profiles. Who is this guy? And what does he want with me?

10:23 AM

It occurs to me that it's a good thing he made me pay for the gas. If Mr. Kozlov comes in and finds me missing, then he could call the cops and they could track me by tracing my bank-card transactions. Right? Like on cop shows on TV. They find people like that all the time.

But the hope doesn't last long. Not even as long as it takes for us to drive across the parking lot and park in front of the scuzzy-looking washrooms.

Who am I kidding?

Mr. Kozlov will find the gas station locked up with my stupid note on the door, and what will he do? He'll make one phone call. To my cell, to fire me.

And as for my phone, it would be a great way to try to get out of this mess, but it is on the floor of the car, somewhere in the backseat. I haven't charged it for almost two weeks, because I can't find the charger and I have no money and my mom is *leaching me a tesson*, as she says. Teaching me a lesson. She won't lend me the money and she won't give it to me either. She thinks I'm irresponsible with my money. And she's absolutely right. Most of my money is in this car. I've spent so much on Vicky, I could've probably saved up for an entire year of college by now. The only other thing I spend my money on is lottery tickets, which I'm not supposed to buy anyway because I'm underage. But I sell them to myself all the time at the gas station. Surprise, surprise, I never win. Maybe two dollars here and there. But not—

"Get out!" Bud jabs the gun at me.

"All right, all right."

"Jesus, are you deaf or what?" he asks.

I guess I'd spaced out when I turned the car off. Can you blame me if I take a few private moments to go over my shitty little life in anticipation for my imminent death?

And then, something occurs to me.

Yes, he is a crazed lunatic, a masked kidnapper.

Yes, he has a gun.

Yes, he's threatened me with the gun.

But you know what?

I'm not really scared. I was at first. But not now. Is that stupid?

We go into the washroom. It's a single. Just one dingy room that stinks of piss. He orders me to go first.

"I don't have to go." Like I could take a piss in front of this guy.

"Might be your last chance for a while."

Why am I not afraid of him now? There's just *something* about him that isn't scary. Either that, or I'm really, really stupid and have watched so much TV that this just isn't real to me.

"Seriously, not going to happen."

"Fine." He backs up to the urinal.

I smile. This should be interesting. How is he going to take a piss AND keep the gun on me at the same time?

"What're you smiling at?" he asks suspiciously.

"Wasn't smiling."

He pauses, like he's taking the time to decide whether or not to argue the point.

"Come closer," he finally says.

I take one step.

"Don't be a jerk. Stand right here." He points to the filthy wall beside the urinal. It looks like it gets used more as a urinal that the porcelain one.

I pause. I think about the door behind me and contemplate running. And

I should. I could probably get someone's attention pretty quick, between the gas bays and the convenience store and the busy road. But I'm curious.

Isn't that sick and twisted? I'm *curious* about what's going to happen next.

Truth is, this is a way more interesting way to spend a Saturday than stuck by the till at the gas station, listening to the easy-listening station loop the same rusty old songs over and over and selling cigarettes to rude people who can't even be bothered to grunt a thank-you.

I stand by the wall, not touching it. I'm not that curious.

"Close your eyes."

"Gladly," I say.

I hear him whiz and do up his fly. And then the sound of running water.

I open my eyes.

He's washing his hands.

I rarely wash my hands, not that I'm thrilled to admit it, but I'm being honest here. Besides, most guys don't wash their hands, so I'm not the only one.

And come on, what crazed gunman takes a moment and *washes his hands*?

He's even using soap from a crusty dispenser that's fallen off the wall and is oozing all over the counter. He has to wipe his hands on his pants because there's no paper towel. He hasn't noticed me watching yet, so I fold my arms and nod in a private moment of satisfaction. My decision is made.

This guy is harmless. Totally and completely harmless.

Chapter Eight

10:58 AM

We get back in the car, and Bud switches his disguise. I'll admit that the ski mask makes him look a little bit freaky. But not really. Not now that I've decided that he's harmless. We get back onto the highway, still heading for the city.

"So, where to?" I try again, this time sounding casual and meaning it.

"Just drive."

"You don't have to wear that thing," I say. "It's got to be hot."

He says nothing. The gun rests in his lap. I glance at it, hoping that this time—because I'm not afraid anymore—it'll look like a fake. But it still looks real. And it's heavy. I can tell by the way he handles it. You can't pretend something like that.

For a brief moment, I doubt my decision. But then I think back to the pansy way he so carefully and thoroughly washed his hands. He's harmless. He's got to be.

"Look, Bud—"

"Don't call me that."

"Then tell me your name, and I'll call you that."

"Right."

"Anyway, I was going to say that I really don't mind driving you wherever. We can forget about the way things started and just consider this a free ride."

54

I let the offer sit for a minute. He says nothing.

"Really, I don't mind. I hated that job anyway."

What he asks next surprises me and proves that he's harmless.

"You think you'll get fired?" There's concern in his voice. Genuine concern. "Sorry, man."

"Don't worry about it."

The conversation dies there for a while, and we carry on, passing exit after exit. I'm starting to enjoy the drive. I roll down my window and let in the fresh air. It's late spring, and everything smells bright green. I turn on the radio, but there's no good music on, despite how often I switch up the channels.

"I used to have an MP3 set up in here, but it got stolen," I say without thinking first. "And the CD changer is stuck on a mix my mom made for me. I put it in to humor her one day when I was driving her to work when her car was in the shop, and the friggin' thing got stuck."

Bud laughs. He actually laughs! I go with it and keep talking. "Like, there's only so much ABBA one can handle, right."

"Without someone thinking you're gay," Bud mutters with another laugh.

"Right." I don't push it, but I really think I'm making progress with this guy. Give it another few miles and I'm going to know everything about him. Most importantly, why the hell he carjacked me at gunpoint.

11:00 AM

But not even half a mile later, there's steam pouring out from under the hood, and the engine starts to splutter.

"You did this on purpose!" Bud protests as I pull onto the shoulder.

"I did not!" I turn the engine off and pop the hood. "When, huh? When could

I have arranged this? Not when we were pulled over by the cop. And not when you made me watch you take a leak!"

"I told you not to watch."

"Whatever," I say as I grab an oil rag off the floor and get out of the car.

"Wait!" Up comes the gun, but even if it is real, I doubt it's loaded. And even it is, he's not going to shoot me. "Where do you think you're going?"

"To fix it."

"You can?" He sounds frantic. "Because if you can't, you have to tell me. I don't have time for this! There's no time!"

"Easy, Bud." He doesn't comment on my name for him this time. "I can fix it. This happens at least once a week. I need a new seal on my radiator cap, but I haven't gotten around to getting one, so I have a rubber band stuck in there. Open the glove box. There's a bag of rubber bands in there. Grab me one."

Traffic zooms by as I lift the hood, steam billowing out.

"And grab that jug of water from the backseat," I yell. I reach for the super-hot cap, rag at the ready. But as I do, my arm catches on a jagged piece of metal. I feel a sudden stab of pain, but ignore it. I always nick myself when I'm farting around in Vicky's engine.

Bud is beside me, looking ridiculous in his ski mask, holding out the rubber band like some lame little peace offering. Maybe someone passing will notice that he looks exactly like what he is, a suspicious dude in a ski mask holding up an innocent guy at the side of the road.

"Thanks." The pain in my arm is insane. So much so that I leave the rad cap on and take a look at what I'm expecting to be a scrape. A bad one, sure, but nothing like what it is. I sliced open my right forearm like I was hell-bent on killing myself. A deep, bloody cut runs halfway from my wrist to my elbow. "Holy shit." I shut my eyes and lean against the car.

I am not good with blood.

"Hold it up." I can feel Bud lifting my arm in the air. "Hang on."

I blink. He reaches into the car and grabs my gym strip off the backseat. He drops the shorts and rips the T-shirt into strips.

"Put pressure on it," he orders. He arranges my other hand over the cut and presses. "Hard."

I do what he says, but I'm feeling dizzy. "I'm going to pass out."

"No, you're not, Zane." Bud pours half the jug of water over the cut. "Relax."

"We need that for the rad!" I manage to say despite the pain.

"There's enough. Slow your breathing down. You're hyperventilating." Then he folds a couple of the shirt strips into a rectangle pad and sets that over the cut, which is still bleeding hard. Then he ties another strip around it, to keep it in place, then the third strip, to add more pressure.

"It's not as bad as it looks. You're not even going to need stitches."

"You're good," I say. "Thanks."

"Cadets," he mumbles as he ties a tidy knot in the final strip of shirt.

So he's in cadets. Do I know anyone who is in cadets? Negatory. At least no one I can think of while struggling to stay standing up instead of passing out in a big lame heap on the side of the highway. That'd be one way to get out of this bizarro field trip. But like I said earlier, I'm curious.

Curious enough to drive despite the pain. Which, I have to admit, isn't so bad now that I can't see any blood.

"You really think I don't need stitches?"

"It's pretty shallow. The way I packaged you up, it'll knit back together okay. You might have a scar though. And you'll need a tetanus shot."

"Nah. I'll be fine. I've had a million tetanus shots in my life."

And then he tells me.

"Well," he says with a definite catch in his throat, "we're going to the hospital anyway, so if you change your mind, you can get a tetanus shot there."

With that, he pulls off his ski mask.

It's Carlyle Dennison, all-around academic wizard, captain of the chess team and grade-eleven mathlete squad, amateur theater buff. I've been kidnapped by my school's biggest and most harmless geek-loser extraordinaire.

Chapter Nine

11:13 AM

Carlyle Dennison. It all begins to make sense.

First of all, he has a girlfriend. Sarita Doud. It may sound weird that such a loser guy has a girlfriend, but when I explain, it will make sense. See, she's just as much a loser as he is.

Okay, that feels weird to say. Like speaking ill of the dead, only she's not dead.

But she's going to be.

She was in a car accident two nights ago, on her way home from rehearsal for one of those hokey musicals they're always trying to get people to audition for. She had the right-of-way at a green light, and some guy who was reaching for his cell phone ran the red light and smashed into her. I saw it on the news. Her car was mashed in half lengthwise. The driver's half. She'd picked up her cat at the vet just before the accident, and they found it in its little travel crate like a whole block away. Purring. But apparently that's what cats do when they're stressed, not just when they're happy.

"How is she?"

Bud—Carlyle—shrugs. "I don't know." He shrugs again, and his voice goes high and warbly. "I don't know! No one will tell me!"

"Which brings us to today's little gun-and-ski-mask adventure?"

He nods. And then he starts crying. Bawling! What do you do when a dude is crying in your car?

Keep asking questions, that's what. Because I want to know how the hell he ever thought it was a good idea to *carjack* someone for a ride.

"Not just someone," he says as he wipes his eyes with the bottom of his shirt. "You. I knew you worked there on Saturdays. And I know you have a car. With tinted windows."

"Ever heard of a friggin' bus?"

"There isn't one until tonight. Don't you think I thought of everything?"

"How about *asking* me, dude?"

"You would've left work to drive me?"

"Okay, no. But you cost me my job!"

"Call him. Tell him you got sick."

I pause. This is actually a good idea. I glance at my watch. Kozlov isn't supposed to be at the station for another forty-five minutes. It might work!

He hands me his cell phone, and I make the call. Mr. Kozlov answers, gruff as usual.

"What?"

"It's Zane," I mumble, working up my sick voice. "I'm sick. I had to leave the station to go to the hospital."

"You left?" He's angry already, and will stay that way. So why drag it out?

"Hang on—" I wretch into the phone. It's so convincing that I almost make myself barf for real.

"Disgusting!" Kozlov groans. "You left the station? No one is there?"

"Correct." I gag again. "I tried to—"

"Okay, okay!" Kozlov cuts me off. "Call me when you are better. I'll cover your shift for tomorrow."

"Thank you, Mr. Kozlov."

He hangs up on me. I turn back to Carlyle. "Good idea."

"Still got your job?"

"I think so." I stare at him until I have to look back at the traffic. "Couldn't you have called one of your friends to give you a ride?"

"What friends?"

It's true. I'd only ever seen him hanging out with Sarita.

"Still, a gun? Come on."

"I have to see her. She might die." This starts him off crying again.

The last I heard, she's most definitely going to die. The gun starts to make a tiny bit of sense.

I turn up the music. He turns his face to the window. We give each other a moment, and then he breaks loose. "I got the bus last night and went to see her. But her family won't let me in her room!"

"Why?"

"Because she's not even allowed to *date*, let alone date a white guy who's not Iranian or Muslim."

"But you guys have been dating forever." Well, at least since grade nine. Which seems like forever. Sarita and Carlyle. Dork devotion defined. Both pimply and awkward, she a little on the chubbified side, he on the scrawny end of skinny. But they're cute, in that share-your-lunch kind of way. And she's nice. Like, genuinely *nice*. No one hates Sarita. No one wants to be her best friend either, but no one disses her. Especially not now.

"But her family doesn't know." Carlyle gulps back a sob. "That's why we're in all that extracurricular stuff together. So we can hang out and her parents won't find out!"

"They know now though?"

He nods miserably. "I went over to her house this morning to beg. Like, on my knees, begging. Like, I actually got on my knees and pleaded with her uncle to let me go see her. He threatened to kill me if I came anywhere near her. Her parents are at the hospital, but her uncle said if her dad had been there he *would've* killed me. Right then! And I guess Ms. Harcourt had called them too and tried to convince them to let me see her. So they know everything now."

"That bitch."

Ms. "Meddle" Harcourt, guidance counselor to the masses.

She loves sticking her nose into your business, and the more chaos she creates, the better, in her mind. It's a make-work project for her, keeping her in business. She gets to tell your mother that you wrote a fictional story for grade-ten English in which the character accuses another character of wanting to kill herself, and Ms. Harcourt gets wind of it and calls your mother and tells her that you're going to commit suicide if something isn't done to stop you. And so you spend ten Tuesday evenings at a psychiatrist's office convincing him that it was fiction, and several more unbearably long "talk times" with Ms. Harcourt trying to convince her that she was wrong all along. Not that I'm bitter or anything.

"I heard about the suicidal thing," Carlyle mutters.

"I never was."

He says nothing.

"I wasn't!" We're nearing the city limits now. "And what I want to know is how that gets out, you know?"

"Uh-huh. Like I want to know how everyone knows that I gave her that cat. I never told anyone."

"I'd heard about that," I said. "And I heard that you stole the cat back, last night."

"I did."

"I respect that. I really do."

"Thanks. They had him locked outside. It was easy."

"I have no idea where the hospital is," I say as we pass a couple of exits that go downtown.

"Two more exits." Carlyle grins. "I know they'd get rid of him when Sarita—" The grin collapses and the tears start again. "When she—"

"Left or right?"

"They hate that cat. Left," he chokes through the tears. And then he makes himself say it, even though I was giving him a perfectly good out. "I know they'll just get rid of him when she dies. I shouldn't have gotten him for her in the first place, but she really wanted him. We both volunteered at the SPCA, and he came in and he was special to her right away. Followed her around, meowing whenever she left. He's old, you know."

"Yeah?" The cat seems like a pretty safe topic. "How old?"

"Ten. And he's blind. And they left him outside after he was in the accident!" Carlyle shakes his head. "He's a good cat. He could still pick Sarita out of a crowd, even though he's blind."

We drive in silence for a few blocks, until my curiosity gets the better of me again. "Where'd you get the gun?" He's got it resting on his thigh again, the barrel pointing away from me now. "It's a prop, right?"

"Nope," he says. "It's real."

"It's real? What the hell, Carlyle? You kidnapped me with a real friggin' gun?"

"It's not loaded."

"All right. Okay. That makes me feel a little better. And where the hell did you get a handgun?"

"My brother."

"Ah." I've heard about his brother. Ryland. The exact opposite of Carlyle.

In juvie for the third time by grade eight, in prison now at the ripe old age of eighteen for his part in a botched… riiiiight…a botched kidnapping! "Is *that* where you got the bright idea to carjack me?"

"Maybe." Carlyle reddens. "Sorry about that, man. I was desperate."

"You're telling me that you don't know a single person who would lend you a car or give you a ride or let you borrow money for a cab."

"That is exactly true.

"Your parents?"

"My mom went with my dad to a convention in Milwaukee. They won't be home for another three days." Here, he pauses. "Although—"

"Although what?"

"My aunt maybe. I could've asked her."

"But instead you decide carjacking me at gunpoint was a better plan."

"I wasn't thinking, man!" He shakes his head. "You don't understand. I was desperate!"

"Jesus, Carlyle. I could still get you in deep shit for this, you know."

"I know." He glances over, his face all blotchy and damp. "But I'm hoping you won't."

"A gun." This time it's my turn to shake my head. "What the hell were you thinking?"

"Like my brother, apparently." His brother is a member of the UV gang, Universal Violations. They kidnapped a Chinese exchange student and held him for ransom because he'd bragged that his father was a multimillionaire development tycoon. Turns out his father works in a cell-phone factory. So, no ransom. The five guys involved all got caught, and they're all waiting for the trial to start.

"I won't. And not because you have

a full academic scholarship for college next year."

"You feel sorry for me?"

"No. Well, yes." I've been following the H signs that point the way to the hospital. Now there's a big sign saying that the hospital is two blocks away. "Of course I feel sorry for you, because of Sarita. But I've had fun, you know?"

"Sure."

"No, really. I'll admit I was scared at first, but that's no different than a wicked roller coaster. It's scary, but fun. You even pay to do it all over again. I haven't had such a good time in a long time."

"Glad one of us is having a good time."

"Sorry, Bud." The nickname slips right off my tongue. "Carlyle."

"I like the name, actually. Call me Bud if you want."

"I'm just glad that I didn't lose my license."

We near the hospital. He pales as the buildings loom, serious, ahead of us.

"What are you going to do, Bud?" I ask.

"See her. By whatever means necessary."

"You can't use the gun. They'll lock down the whole hospital and bring in the SWAT team."

"I have to see Sarita." Carlyle—Bud—grips the gun in his hand, his knuckles white, as I pull into the parking lot. "If I can carjack you at gunpoint and make you believe it, then I can get in to see her. Whatever it takes."

Chapter Ten

12:06 PM

What do I do now? What if he pulls the crazed-gunman act again? And in a *hospital*!

That's the kind of thing that gets the SWAT-team sniper nailing you with the laser scope just before they take you down with one ace shot from way up on a rooftop somewhere.

I should go home.

"You can go," Bud says, as if I'd said the words out loud.

"Well"—I pull the car into a parking spot—"I could."

I should.

I really should.

Don't be an idiot, Zane. I can hear my mother lecturing me. Come home. Come *home*. "I should call my mom, at least. Let her know that I'm okay."

"I can do this on my own." Bud slides the gun into his waistband and gets out of the car.

Now what?

Go with him on what could be the biggest adventure of my life so far, or go home and face Mr. Kozlov? I'd have to make up some wicked story to keep my job. I'd have to tell him something crazy, like I'd been carjacked at gunpoint and forced to drive some lunatic to the city.

As if he'd believe me.

"We need to pay for the parking, if you're going to stay." Bud gives me a guilty look. "I don't have any money."

"Uh, right." I have to make a decision. "Give me your phone."

He hands me his phone, and I dial home. It rings and rings, and then goes to the voice mail. "Hey, Mom. If Mr. Kozlov calls to check on me, just tell him I'm in bed, too sick to come to the phone. I'll explain later. See ya." I flip the phone shut.

"So?" Bud gets out of the car and leans back in. "You in, or out?"

"I'm in." I shake my head, mystified at myself. "Stupid as it sounds, I'm in."

The info-desk lady tells us that Sarita is in the Intensive Care Unit on the fifth floor.

"You want some lunch or something?" I'm getting nervous as we get closer to when Bud might go ballistic. I kind of want to buy some time.

"Are you kidding?" Bud frowns. "I want to see Sarita. That's it. I don't want anything else. Get it?"

For a second, I catch a glimpse of the guy that had me so scared for so long.

"Right, okay. Sorry. Let's go." I head for the elevator, and he follows.

We get on, and he pushes the button to the second floor.

A family crowds onto the elevator just as the doors are about to close. A mom and dad, a grandpa, two little kids who are arguing over who gets to push the buttons, and a baby zonked out in a stroller, his head lolled to one side, drool hanging off his chin.

It's a short ride, but it's long enough for me to wonder how it is possible that those everyday people in that everyday elevator on this everyday Saturday in an everyday hospital can have *no* idea that they're within arm's reach of a gun and a kid not afraid to use it…even if it isn't loaded. I can sense Bud's tension as the kids keep bickering. He's staring at the floor numbers, and when five lights up, he pushes his way to the door and stumbles out as if he'd been pushed from behind.

He leans over and plants his hands on his knees and takes a deep breath.

"I get claustrophobic," he gasps. "Should've taken the stairs."

"You all right now?"

"Yeah." He straightens. "Let's do this."

We look at the signs and follow the ones that lead to the ICU. When we get there, there are two heavy doors closing the hallway off from the ICU and a little intercom off to one side. Above it is a sign telling us to use the intercom to check in.

Already, I can tell this is not going to be pretty.

Or easy.

"Now what?" I ask.

As an answer, Bud presses the button on the intercom.

"*ICU*," the voice says.

"Uh, hi…I'm here to see Sarita?"

"*Who?*"

"Sarita Doud," Bud says. "D-O-U-D."

"*Hold, please.*"

Bud pales. "What if we're too late?"

I'm just starting to wonder that myself. "I'm sure…" I'm sure of what? That his girlfriend isn't dead? Not in the least. Thankfully the voice over the intercom interrupts me from having to come up with something to say.

"*And you are?*" the voice asks in a sharp, nasally tone.

"Her boyfriend. Carlyle Dennison." There's a long pause. Carlyle panics. I can see it in his face. "Look, I know I'm not on her list or whatever, but I have to see her. I have to!"

Another pause, and then the voice speaks. "*I'm sorry, hon, but unless you're on the family's approved list, I can't let you in.*"

"Please." Bud leans his head against the wall beside the intercom. His finger pressing the intercom button is shaking. "Please, please, please, please let me see her. Even just for two seconds. Please, please, please, please…"

"*I can go check with her parents, see if they'll add you to the list.*"

"No!" Bud shakes his head, his forehead still pressed against the wall. "No. You don't understand. They hate me—"

"*I'm sorry. There's nothing I can do.*" The woman on the other end of the intercom sounds genuinely sorry. "*You'll have to make arrangements with the family to be allowed to see her.*"

Bud starts crying. Maybe this will soften the intercom lady up even more.

"Can you tell me how she is? Can you tell me that?"

"*Sorry, I can't disclose patient information. I'm sorry. Good luck.*" And then there's a click, and she's gone.

"No!" Bud bangs his head against the wall. "No!" He stabs the intercom button over and over until the women's voice comes back, this time annoyed.

"*ICU, can I help you?*" She knows it's us. Or Bud.

"Please, you have to help me! I have to see her."

"*I understand that you're upset, but if you persist in trying to access the ICU, I'll have to call security to have you removed from hospital grounds. Understand?*"

Bud tries pushing the doors open, but they don't budge. I yank him away and say into the intercom. "We understand. Sorry."

Bud reaches into his waistband and takes out his gun. I glance up, looking for cameras. I don't think there are any, just the intercom.

"Think this through!" I say in a stern whisper, not wanting anyone in the waiting room across the hall to hear us. "This isn't the way to get in to see her!"

"Then how?" Bud yells, holding onto his gun with both hands.

"Not like this." I make a grab for it again. "Gimme that."

Sure enough, a little girl comes out of the waiting room and stares up at us as I try to wrestle the gun from him one more time.

"What are you doing?" she asks, a coloring book dangling from one hand and a teddy bear tucked under her other arm.

Bud slips the gun behind his back. "Nothing."

"You were fighting." The little girl frowns at us. She must be about six. "There's no fighting allowed here. It's a rule."

"Thanks," I say. "Better go back to your mommy and finish coloring your picture now, kid."

"My mommy's in there." She points to the ICU doors. "She's sick."

Bud and I share a look. Poor kid.

"She was flopping on the floor and I called nine-one-one and the anblanse brought her here. They brought me too, and the man gave me this teddy."

"Ambulance," I correct her.

"Uh-huh."

"Look," I whisper to Bud. "Let's go make a plan. Okay? This one obviously isn't working."

"A plan for what?" the little girl asks.

"To see my girlfriend."

"She's in there?"

Bud nods and then starts crying again. I really don't know what to do when he does this, so I shuffle the girl back into the waiting room and leave him in the hall with himself. "Don't—and I mean *do not*—do anything stupid," I say over my shoulder.

The waiting room is empty. The little girl has dumped a toy box full of junky hospital waiting-room toys onto the table.

"There's nothing good to play with," she says. " 'Cept the lady brought me crayons." And she goes back to work, coloring a picture of a circus elephant in her book.

Bud appears at the door. "So?"

"What?"

"What plan do you have?"

I stare at him. "It's been twenty seconds. Give me a minute or two."

He sits across from me, and we both watch the little girl color. She's working hard, her tongue wedged between her lips, shoulders hunched in concentration.

"What about dressing up as a cleaner?" Bud suggests in a whisper. "I could find the staff room and steal a uniform, you know?"

"The staff room will be locked. Are you kidding?"

Bud sits there, his knee jiggling. He chews on a fingernail. "Or I could be the flower delivery guy."

This doesn't seem like such a bad idea. "You might be on to something there."

"You think?"

"Yeah."

"Okay." A new hope spreads across his face. I really hope this works, because I don't know how long I can keep him from using that damn gun.

Chapter Eleven

12:28 PM
We go in search of flowers, ending up in the cancer ward.

Yes, we're going to steal them from cancer patients.

It's an interesting kind of low, but one that we decided was okay, being that Sarita was also dying, and Bud is very literally also dying…to see her.

"It is like dying," he says as we make our way down a dim, quiet corridor. "Like part of me will go with her."

I'm not so sure that dying people would have much empathy for his comparison, but I don't argue. I'm trying to look casual, like we're going to visit a favorite uncle. Bud gave me a bit of acting coaching in the elevator.

"It's all in the shoulders," he said. "Relax. If you're tense, they'll know that you have no reason to be there."

Remembering this, I pull my shoulders down from my ears, where they were parked, fixed with tension.

"We need to find a private room," Bud says as he comes back from peeking into yet another ward room, four beds, each with an old man camped out with an accompanying doting wife, both of them watching the little TV pulled down in front of them. "Or at least a room where all the other people are asleep."

12:33 PM

We find the perfect room at the very end of the hall, a large private suite with a view of the city and one shriveled old lady asleep in the bed, propped up with her mouth gaping open.

"Bingo," I say.

Bud leans tentatively into the room. "Is she alive?"

Just then she lets out a little snort.

"Yep," I say. "Let's get this over with. This isn't exactly my proudest moment. My mother would disown me."

We tiptoe past her bed. She looks about a hundred years old, but that could just be the cancer. The bedside table and ledge below the window are both lined with vases of flowers. All shapes and sizes of arrangements, every kind of stinky flower you can imagine. In fact, the place smells like a nasty cross between a perfume factory and a medicine cabinet.

"That one," Bud whispers. He's reaching down for the biggest arrangement of all. It's a basket so large it has to sit on the floor. The flowers and greenery reach up to his waist in an elaborate fan of reds and pinks. "She loves pink."

The absurdity of the whole day sets me off. I let loose with the kind of laughter better left to really, really good live comedy.

"Shut up!" Bud eyes me hard.

We both look at the bed. The old lady keeps snoring, her bottom lip quivering a little with each snore. That just makes me laugh harder. I try to laugh silently but I just get the hiccups, which are just as loud.

The old lady stirs. Still sleeping, her jaw clacks shut and her brow furrows.

"Let's go. Let's go!" Bud reaches for the flowers, which are obviously as heavy as they look. He drags the huge basket halfway across the room while

I wrestle with my uncontrollable laughter and equally uncontrollable hiccups. I lean over, grasp my knees and hold my breath. That sometimes works for the hiccups.

"Help me out here, would you?" Bud doesn't whisper this. He practically yells it. The old lady's eyes snap open.

"Hello?" She pushes herself up on bony elbows. She locks her watery eyes on me. "Larry?"

"Uh, no." I look around for somewhere to hide, but she's not letting me out of her sight.

"Larry! Get over here and give me a kiss before you sneak off to work. I packed your lunch." She struggles to sit up and reaches for a bunch of wadded-up, crusty tissues.

"Whatever it takes," Bud growls, glaring at me. He drags the huge basket of flowers another few feet toward the door.

She points an arthritic finger at Bud. "Where's Greg going with those tires?"

Okay, so she's obviously loopy.

Bud/Carlyle/Greg doesn't miss a beat. "Switching them for the dud ones."

"Okay." She settles back against the pillows. "But you tell your father there that he is not allowed to leave without giving me a kiss."

"Aw, come on, Dad." Bud grins at me. "Give Ma a kiss. For good luck."

I am frozen where I stand. There is no way that I'm going to kiss that dying old lady we're stealing flowers from.

"If you don't kiss me right this minute," she says with a sly smile, "I will scream."

"Kiss her, Dad." Bud mouths *please*. "We gotta get going." He really is a good actor.

I tell myself this is kind of like acting too. I approach the bed, breathing through my mouth to stave off the hospital reek.

"Right here," she taps her lips.

"Sorry, darling." I peck her quickly on her papery cheek. "Don't want to give you my cold, now, do I?" I know I sound like a retard. I'd lowered my voice and said the words as if reading them awkwardly off a teleprompter. But it seems to do the trick. She pats my arm and smiles a great big toothless smile.

"That's all right dear. Now off you go, don't let Greg do those tires all by himself."

"Thanks, Ma!" Bud/Carlyle/Greg actually kisses her too, on the cheek. "I owe you one."

12:41 PM

It takes both of us to carry the massive flower arrangement back up to the ICU.

"Those are nice," the little girl says as she peeks out of the waiting room.

"Thanks," Bud says. "They're for my girlfriend."

"Why's she in there?" As the little girl says this, the heavy doors swing open and a nurse comes out. "Is she really sick too?"

"No flowers in the ICU," the nurse says as she breezes past, her shoes squeaking efficiently on the linoleum.

In the second it takes Bud to process this, the doors close with a hydraulic sigh.

He drops his end of the basket, and I drop mine. The basket lands on the floor with a thud, along with our stupid plan.

And Bud/Carlyle's heart, and his sad-ass self. Literally. He slides down the wall and lands on the floor beside the basket of flowers. He drops his head in his hands and starts crying.

Chapter Twelve

12:52 PM

"It's okay." The little girl hands Bud the picture of the elephant she's colored and ripped carefully from the coloring book. "Don't cry."

"Thanks—" He checks the picture for her name. Sure enough, she's signed it in big crayon letters. Mia. "Thanks, Mia."

"You're welcome."

Bud wipes his eyes with his shirt and stands up with so much effort he looks like he belongs in the ICU.

He's still got the gun tucked in his waistband. I catch a glimpse of it when he wipes his eyes again, lifting his shirt higher this time. Thankfully, the little girl didn't see it, or didn't know what she was looking at, if she did.

"I need to talk to you," Bud says to me in a flat tone.

This is going to be about the gun. And how he's going to use it to get in there and see Sarita. I have to think fast. I glance into the waiting room. There's a few more people in there, although no one seems attached to Mia.

"Not in there," I say. Then I remember the basket of flowers. "Let's take the flowers back. You can tell me what's on your mind on the way."

Bud's hand drifts to the gun. His fingers find the handle, tighten around it.

"Bud!" I say forcefully. Mia flinches.

Bud glares at me. "We tried it your way."

"Hey, Mia." I kneel down to talk to her. "How about you go back into the waiting room and color me a picture?"

She glances warily at Bud. "Is he okay?"

"He will be." I push her gently toward the waiting room.

"Bud," I say again. He doesn't break his creepy stare. "Carlyle!"

"What?" he finally says. "Got another great idea?"

"We're taking the flowers back," I say firmly. "Now."

"What if there's no time?"

"There's time."

"You don't know that."

"We could be there and back by now." I grab one end of the heavy basket. "Let's go. Now."

He grabs the other end, and we make our way back to the cancer ward.

But Bud doesn't want to talk on the way there. He walks fast, making me drop my end twice before we even get to the elevator. This time the old lady stays asleep, and we're in and out of her room in seconds.

1:03 PM

On the way back, he tells me how it's going to go.

"I'm going to use you as a hostage," he says. "I only need a minute with her; then I'll give up."

"The whole hospital will get locked down. There'll be SWAT guys all over the place."

"They won't even be here before I give up." He's talking like he's making simple plans to go to a football game, or in his case, the theater. This is probably just another play to him. Something to act out. Something to pretend.

But his wanting to see Sarita is real. And I sympathize.

"But I can't go along with it," I say. "I can't get arrested. No way."

"I'll say I forced you."

We're back at the waiting room, which has emptied out. Except for Mia, who's sitting in the hall, rolling a small rubber ball back and forth.

"I waited for you." She rolls the ball again. "They told me I can't bounce it because it's disruptive." She checks to make sure the ICU doors are closed before showing us. She bounces the ball off the wall. It makes a tiny *whack* sound. "See? I don't think it's loud."

"I guess they're picky," I say.

It occurs to me that she is very young to be all alone, and all this time we've been here, no one has checked on her.

"Who's in there with your mom?" I ask.

Bud glares at me and taps his watch. I get it. He wants to get on his idiotic plan. I hold up my hand, gesturing for him to wait a minute.

"No one."

"Who's hanging out here with you?"

"You guys." She shrugs. "I guess."

"Besides us, I mean."

"No one." Another shrug. "I don't need a babysitter. Besides, my big brothers are coming. Then I can go in."

This gets Bud's attention. He squats down. "How old are they?"

"Old."

"Older than us?"

"I guess."

Bud sits cross-legged in front of her, and they roll the ball back and forth between them. "Do they go to high school?"

Mia shakes her head. "No, silly."

"Do they go to college?"

"Anthony goes to cooking school, where he learns how to make candy and cook turkeys."

"What about your other brother?" Bud glances up at me, eyes bright.

"He's a daddy. He's got a baby girl. I'm an auntie!" Mia grins. "Auntie Mia. Jesse is coming on a plane, but he's not bringing anyone. Just himself. To see Mommy."

I know exactly where this is going.

"How would you like to see your mommy before your brothers get here?"

Mia jumps up. "Can I?"

"Sure." Bud asks me if I'm in with a silent questioning glance. I nod, not altogether convinced. At least he's forgotten his insane hostage idea. "Yes. Here's how."

Chapter Thirteen

1:10 PM
Mia, it turns out, is a little Hollywood star in the making. Once she understands how we're going to do this, she marches right up to the intercom and buzzes the ICU.

"*ICU.*"

"Hi, this is Mia Kellerman. My brothers are here now."

They've been expecting this and let us in without another question.

Bud's eyes light up for a second, and then he's back in his role as Anthony. His expression is both anxious and controlled. His jaw flexes from the clenching. He grips Mia's hand as if he really is her older brother.

He is a good actor, I'll give him that. He's gone from crazed gunman to doting son to responsible older brother in the course of a few hours. I've been told to keep my mouth shut and act like I'm babysitting Mia.

As we make our way into the dimly lit hall of the ICU, I take Mia's other hand, not sure what else to do.

Bud/Carlyle/Greg/Anthony marches us right up to the nurses' station.

"We're here to see Anita Kellerman. I'm her son Anthony. This is my brother Jesse, and you've met Mia."

The nurse glances up. "She's in bed

three-oh-five. Her nurse will fill you in on how she's doing." She gives us all a warm smile and returns to her work.

My job is to check if there's a board, like on TV, where all the patients are listed. There is. Sarita Doud, bed 308. There's also a row of clipboards wedged into stands, and one of them has DOUD written across the top. I check to make sure the nurse is not looking, and then I lift the clipboard and tuck it under my shirt.

Bud might make the better actor, but I make the better criminal. Years of stealing from the corner store at the end of my block have not gone to waste. It's a skill, man.

Mia and Bud lead the way. We deliberately overshoot the room, so that we can see what's going on in Sarita's room.

As soon as he gets within sight of her, his act is over. He visibly slumps and lets out a whimper.

"Bed three-oh-five." The same nurse sees that we've missed it. "This one." She points to the door across from the nurses' station.

"Thanks," I say.

Sarita looks terrible. There are more tubes than I've ever seen in a television ICU, and more machines than I saw in the cancer ward. The room is dimly lit, with a soft light behind her bed casting a gloomy shadow over her. Her mouth is wedged open by a breathing tube, and her eyes are raccooned in bruises, the left one so swollen that it doesn't look like an eye anymore. One leg is in a full cast, propped up with a bunch of foam wedges, and one of her hands is strapped to a splint.

Her parents flank her, one on either side of the bed, heads bent to the sheets, praying silently.

They don't look like the mean parents Bud described. They just look sad. Really, really sad.

"Sarita," Bud whispers. "Oh no. No."

"Thank you," I say again, shoving Bud ahead of me. Mia has run ahead and is already in the room. Her mother's nurse stops her from leaping up onto the bed.

"Walk." I shove Bud again. "You're Anthony, older brother to Mia," I whisper. "Act like it!"

He snaps out of it. "Mia," he says sternly as we get to the room. "Wait. Mom might not be able to hug you right now."

"You two must be Anthony and Jesse." The nurse rises to greet us. She'd been perched on a stool, recording something in Mrs. Kellerman's chart. "We weren't expecting you until later."

And then Anita Kellerman turns her head and looks at us with clear, confused eyes. She reaches for her daughter, and Mia hugs her gently.

"Much later," she says over Mia's shoulder. Mia, suddenly uncomfortable and scared, clings to her mother for a long while. Bud and I stand there, dumbfounded. We hadn't thought Mrs. Kellerman would be conscious. Or I hadn't. I'd told Bud that everyone in the ICU was unconscious. I'd said, very confidently, that you *had* to be unconscious to be in the ICU.

Guess not.

"Mom," Anthony says with a catch in his throat. It's believable, even though I know the near tears are for Sarita, or perhaps the realization that we're going to get kicked out.

But Mrs. Kellerman gives us a chance. "Beverly?" The nurse looks up. "Can you give us a minute, alone?"

"Of course."

1:18 PM

We explain everything. And to our relief, Mrs. Kellerman doesn't rat us out.

"I'm just glad to see Mia," she says. "The boys' flights don't get in until tonight."

Bud drifts anxiously toward the door. He leans out and glances down the hall.

"How is he going to get in there?" Mrs. Kellerman asks me.

I shrug. "He'll find a way, trust me."

1:25 PM

And it doesn't take long.

"Come with me," he says to me as he heads out of Mrs. Kellerman's room.

He passes Sarita's room without even so much as a look toward the door. This is how I know he has a pretty solid plan. He grabs something off a linen cart and disappears into the washroom at the end of the hall. When he emerges, he's wearing a hospital gown. And that's it. Nothing else. He grabs an IV pole that has bag set up, ready to use. He tucks the tubing down the front of his gown and clutches the pole as he hobbles toward me.

"I'm Jason Renville, president of the student union. You're my brother Miles. Steady me." I can barely grab his elbow and pretend to help him before he's limped into Sarita's room and right up to the foot of her bed.

"Mr. and Mrs. Doud," he says in a politely hushed voice. "I'm Jason Renville, president of the student union."

Of course, they don't know what Bud looks like because he's never been allowed to meet them. This is working in his favor right now.

"I know there are no visitors allowed," he says as Sarita's parents lift their teary eyes from their daughter. "But I'm also a patient in this unit, and the students at school really wanted me to pass along their best wishes in person. I hope you don't mind."

"Thank you," Mr. Doud says. "Are you a friend of Sarita's?"

"I can't say that I know her very well myself." He really is a brilliant actor. Bud/Carlyle/Greg/Anthony/Jason nods and smiles like a seasoned politician. "But so many of her fellow classmates have nothing but good things to say about her."

"Yes?" Mrs. Doud wants to know specifics.

"Your Sarita is smart, and funny, and kind and caring, and generous and very beautiful."

I start to think he's pushing it with the "beautiful" bit, but her parents obviously agree, because they're nodding, both of them with tears streaming down their faces.

All of a sudden, Beverly is at the door. But she doesn't yank us out of there. Instead she leans into the room, eyes on the Douds. "Your family is in the waiting room. They'd like to speak to the two of you. It's time for Sarita's bed bath, so you can come back in a little while."

"Oh," Mr. Doud says. "All right."

"Please be brief," Mrs. Doud says. "I want to be with her."

"You'll just be through the ICU doors, only steps away. We'll call you back in if we need to."

Mr. and Mrs. Doud stand, and perhaps because they're on autopilot and need to be told what to do, or maybe because to them a nurse's word is law, they both leave the room. I'm sure they could've stayed if they'd known to insist.

They both kiss Sarita, one parent on each cheek.

"Thank you," Mr. Doud says. "Thank you for coming to see our Sarita. Perhaps you can tell her that her friends miss her and can't wait for her to come back to school." His accent makes the words sound like a singsong. "We are so looking forward to her coming home. You tell the school that. We await the return of her good health."

With that, her parents take each other's hand and leave the room, fully expecting us to leave as well.

Beverly cuts the two of us with a glare. "Mrs. Kellerman told me what you're up to, and I don't like it one bit." The scolding comes out in a harsh, whispered flurry. "But I feel sorry for you, which might be stupid, so I'm giving you two minutes. *Two minutes* and then you get the hell off my ward. Understood?"

"Yes, ma'am," Bud says. "Thank you! Thank you!"

"Sarita?" The nurse leans over her. "Are you awake?"

I wonder why she's asking a dying girl if she's awake. But then Sarita opens her one good eye. Her gaze rests on the nurse for a second, and then she sees Carlyle. She smiles. Even with the breathing tube, I can tell she's smiling. It's all over her ravaged face.

"Sarita!" He rushes to her side, taking her one good hand in his. He kisses the back of it, gently.

I back out of the room and leave him alone with her. I bump into Beverly in the hallway.

"It so happens that some of their family *is* in the waiting room, so hopefully this ends with none of them the wiser."

"Thank you," I say. "He's been so upset not to be able to—"

"Save it," she says. "You can thank me by getting out of here and leaving me with my job intact." She stalks off, but I call after her.

"Wait!"

She stops. "What is it?"

"Is she going to be okay?"

"With a lot of time and a lot of healing, yes."

"Really?"

"It was touch and go for a while, but she's going to make it."

"Wow." I shake my head. "Everyone at school thinks she's dying." I glance behind me into the room, where Carlyle is leaning over Sarita, grinning, tears running down his face. "He thought she was too."

1:38 PM

So Sarita will live. I keep an eye on Bud through the window, not because I'm curious or nosy, but so that I can play interference should the need arise. He leans over the bed and kisses her on the lips. He strokes her lank hair and whispers to her. I can't imagine what he's saying, and I don't really want to know. It's between him and Sarita.

I can see the machines from where I stand. Her heart rate goes up while he talks to her. It goes up even more when he kisses her good-bye and backs out of the room, his face awash in tears. His tears slow, and a smile erupts across his face when I tell him what the nurse said. He makes her tell him in her own words.

"You swear it?" He presses her. "You promise she'll be okay?"

"I never make promises." Beverly peers at us from the other side of the counter. "But she is going to be fine. A little worse for wear maybe. Perhaps a lot worse for wear, but she's going to make it."

Chapter Fourteen

1:49 PM
Still grinning ear to ear, Bud changes back into his clothes, and we say a quick good-bye and thank-you to Mia and her mother. While we're in Mrs. Kellerman's room, the Douds return to Sarita's, so I'm not worried about getting caught on the way out.

On our way to the elevator, we have to pass the ICU waiting room. Sarita's family takes up three long couches. A large man leaps up as we pass.

"Shit!" Bud grips my arm. "Let's go!"

"What?" I follow him at a run.

"Stop!" The man is running after us.

"That's her uncle!" Bud jabs at the elevator Down button. He looks for the stairs. "The one who threatened to kill me!"

"Over there." The stairs are at the far end of the hall, marked by an Emergency Exit sign.

Sarita's uncle and three other guys from her family chase us all the way to the stairs. I get there first and yank the door open. But Sarita's uncle grabs Bud by the back of his shirt and spins him around.

"What the hell are you doing here?" He doesn't wait for an answer though.

Instead he slams Bud against the wall and punches him square in the face.

"Stop!" A hospital security guard is running toward us, yelling into his shoulder mike for backup.

Another punch.

Bud groans.

"Stop!"

Sarita's thugs finally notice the guard and hesitate long enough for us to start down the stairs. We're on the first landing before I look back. No one is following us.

"Keep going!" I say as Bud slows down. There's a trail of his blood behind us. His nose is gushing, and his lip is cut. "They could still be coming."

We get out of the stairwell on the second floor and take the elevator down. We go past the main floor and all the way to the parking level, even though we parked in an outside lot.

"They won't find us now," I say as we walk between rows of cars. "You okay?"

"Yeah." Bud looks up with a great big bloody grin. "Much better now. Sarita's going to be okay. I can't believe it." He lets out a victorious whoop. "She's going to be okay!"

Chapter Fifteen

Eight weeks later and Sarita is still in the hospital. It's a Saturday, and I'm at the gas station again. Kozlov bought my story about being sick, even though he threatened to fire me for "abandoning my post," as he puts it. Dorkus Roboticus doesn't work here anymore. He vanished. Just stopped showing up. This made Kozlov forget about my transgression pretty quick. Especially when the accountant showed him some very funky numbers. Looks like Dorkus was selling cigarettes and pocketing the money.

Bud thinks Dorkus probably does this on a regular basis, gets hired and then starts helping himself to the cash. We told Sarita all about the Dorkus drama, and she thinks he's probably a drug addict who has to steal to buy drugs. I don't know about that. Dorkus had more to him than I thought, but I doubt he's that complex. He probably steals to support his crossword habit.

What still doesn't add up is why Bud carjacked me. If it had been me, I'd have hitchhiked. Sarita says he should've waited for the bus, or begged his aunt. Bud maintains he had no other choice. He had to get to Sarita fast.

"I just couldn't see any other way, man." He tells me again as I pass off to the newbie nightshift guy. He's shaping up to be Dorkus Roboticus the second, although he won't get away with anything because Kozlov has actually fixed the inside surveillance. Never mind we could've been murdered by a robber off the street, he never got it fixed before. But now that his employees "are all damned thieves," Kozlov got it fixed. "I can't explain it any more than that. You just don't understand."

"Nope." We get into Vicky and head for the highway. "But whatever, Bud. I'm glad you did it."

"What?"

"I'm glad you carjacked me. It was one of the best days of my life. Seriously." I give him a serious frown. "But I wouldn't suggest you ever pull a stunt like that again. Nobody else would be an idiot like me and think it was fun."

"Roger that."

He can't pull the same stunt anyway.

I got rid of the gun. I made him give it to me after that day at the hospital. I took it to the police department and told them I found it behind the gas station when I went to take out the garbage. No more gun.

We're going to see Sarita. This time it's almost okay with her parents, as it has been three times a week for the last eight weeks. They still don't like Carlyle/Bud, but seeing that the hospital is like one big chaperone, they let him see her there.

"How much longer?" I ask.

Bud knows exactly what I'm talking about. He's been counting down the days. "Six more sleeps." But not until she comes home. Six more days until she gets moved to the rehab center only ten minutes away from Bud's house. She still has to learn to walk again, and her left hand is still pretty useless, so she'll be there for a long time.

Who knows if Sarita's family will let them see each other when she finally comes home? Ms. Harcourt has been working on it. She's the one responsible for smoothing over the scene at the hospital. Turns out that she actually knows a thing or two. Turns out she really knows how to talk to parents. Turns out she's not so bad after all.

Bud is doing his part too. He's put his amazing acting skills to use to be the chaste, sweet, studious boy her parents want for her. He's not converting to Islam, but he is doing pretty much everything else to get in their good books.

And me, I'm doing my part by driving Bud into the city three times a week so he can see his girlfriend. Why am I doing this? Partly because I'm curious as to how it will all turn out. But mostly because Bud/Carlyle/Greg/Anthony/Jason is the first real best friend I've ever had. Weird to say that about the guy who held a gun to my head. Weird but true.

Carrie Mac is the best-selling author of *The Beckoners*, *Charmed*, *Crush* and *Pain and Wastings*. Carrie lives in Vancouver, British Columbia.